Enchanted Dreams

Aarna Gupta

Become
Shakespeare
.com

Acknowledgements

I would like to thank my parents and grandparents for always keeping me motivated and inspired. They have helped me in every step of my life and I am very grateful to them. I would also like to acknowledge my school, Step by Step, Noida, and my teachers, as they have made me what I am today and I would like to dedicate the book to them. They have had a big hand throughout this journey and I am very thankful to them.

Author's Descripiton

The author of this book is Aarna Gupta. She is a 12-year-old girl and studies at the *Step by Step School, Noida.* Aarna has had a passion for writing since she was a child and also loves reading. She has penned down her imagination in the form of this book for everyone to read.

Table Of Contents

1. THE WORLD OF MONSTERVILLE

2. HOME SWEET HOME

3. HUARO – THE HALF-HUMAN AND HALF-DINOSAUR

4. MIX-UP

5. NO LOGIC, ONLY MAGIC!

6. DREAMS

7. MY LIFE

8. BOOK LOVER FOREVER

THE WORLD OF MONSTERVILLE

(Axci starts writing in his diary early in the morning)

This is the story of my world - Monsterville.

I am Axci, and I am the son of Wopli and Sedra, and I also have a little sister named Retedu. My family and I live in the city of Yuxciel.

Well, I am pretty sure you must be confused about what I am talking about right now, so let me take you around my world - Monsterville.

What lies beneath is the world of humankind, but above it is our world, Monsterville, which rests upon the clouds. This world came into being because God had told a hippo that he was tired of his job and duties, so God asked the hippo to take up his job and fulfil his duties, and he gave the hippo all his powers by trusting him. From that day on, he became the mighty, majestic and magical hippo from being just a hippo. The hippo was very happy. But as soon as he was given the powers, he created his own world, Monsterville. And that was the start of my world. But day by day, he became more greedy and he started to misuse his powers to kill humans on Earth and to turn them into monsters. Monsterville came alive! So now, he and the other monsters kept killing humans and turned them into monsters. When God got to know about this, he went to the hippo and told him to stop what he was doing. But as the hippo was very notorious and greedy, he made God his slave. Since God had given him all his powers, he was unable to do anything. The hippo now rested on the golden emblem of powers and he was the one who kept all of us alive; hence, he was our god. All of us monsters were immortal but only unless and until the hippo didn't move from its place, for if he did, then all the powers would go back to God and this world would be finished forever; turning us back into humans. But it was impossible to move the hippo from the golden emblem and not even a genius could do that.

Now let me take you for a tour through my world. Our world is very different from the human world. In fact, I can say that our world is its opposite. Here is how it is! In Monsterville, there are 4 cities -

XALIAR

ROCAT

ANOMATA

YUXCIEL (my city)

In my world, everything is done with the help of machines. For instance, preparing food is done through the help of machines and even my school is conducted through the help of machines. Well, speaking of school, we are currently learning about our mother tongue – RETSNOM, and we also learn HSILGNE and THAM. These subjects are basically like English and Math in the human world.

 Let me tell you a little bit about the cities. Every monster who is 20 years old or above, has to work. Every monster has the same job - human fishing. The office or headquarters are the clouds. In this job, the monsters have to kill humans and turn them into monsters. The monsters are also paid money for doing this. Basically, we have our own currency which is 1 water droplet= 1 mon. Mon is the name of our currency. For every human that you turn into a monster, you are paid 10 droplets of water or 10 mon. Everything that you want to purchase has to be bought through the droplets of water only. Even my house is bought through water droplets. Basically, all of us monsters live on clouds and make that our home, but we have to buy them. My house costs 11 water droplets or 11 mon. And more the water droplets that you add to your cloud, the bigger it gets. Everybody has the same job, except for a few people. Each city has 2 idiots. These idiots are extremely smart and are the ones who make the machines. Every city makes different kind of machines and these are exported all over Monsterville. And these idiots are paid a huge amount of water money or mon.

These are just a part of the many surprises at Monsterville. But now, you better get seated because this ride is about to get a little bumpy. Let me introduce you to my favourite thing - food. My favourite dish is fried eye with roasted liver. Yummy. And our city is also famous for burnt kidney with just a hint of gallbladder juice. My mouth is watering, just saying that! But unfortunately, we only get that dish on special occasions like STER-A-CRAY, HIPPARA AND DANNER. Ster-a-cray is basically like birthday in the human world and Hippara is the day when all of us monsters pray to or worship our God - the magical, majestic and mighty hippo, who rests on the golden emblem. That is an auspicious day for all of us monsters. Then, Danner is the day when every monster attends a celebration for who and what they are. We just party all day. It's monstalicious!

Monsterville is wonderful. It's just a small little world that we monsters have made for ourselves. As much as I like living in Monsterville, I also hate what the monsters do to the humans. They practically kill them and force them to be something that they are not and don't want to be. It's unfair, but they don't even realise it. I just wish that their ways and thoughts would change and for once they would act like they have a heart, or that this world would just end and everything would go back to the way it was earlier, when there were no monsters and only humans.

But for that to happen, somebody will have to

move the magic hippo from its place, which is impossible!

(After a tiring day, Axci went back to his room and started writing in his diary again.)

So, today, while I went shopping, I ran into a very old man. He kept on murmuring, "I need to kill these monsters and finish their world."

I think he was saying all of this in Hsilgne. I am not so good at it. Let me just check on the monole. We can search for anything on Monole. Ok, so it means that he wants to kill all of us and wants to destroy our world. Oh no!!

I have to do something. Where does he live? Yes, found it! But he lives in Xaliar. I will take the NIART which is a train, in Hislgne.

(After a few hours Axci reached Xaliar.)

(Axci reaches the old man's house and knocks on the door, and the old man opens the door.)

AXCI: Hi,I am actually Axci. I ran into you at the market and I heard you whispering that you will kill all the monsters and destroy this world, so I have come to talk to you about it.

OLD MAN: Why do you care?

AXCI: I know that I am a monster, but I am not at all pleased with how monsters treat the humans. I have been trying to do something but I have failed to do so.

OLD MAN: I do not trust you.

AXCI: I have thought of a plan and I have made a small document on it. The document is stored in this drive. I shall give you the drive and tell you the plan, if you trust me then we will work together otherwise you have my drive. I will not betray you.

(Axci hands the drive with the document to the old man.)

OLD MAN: Ok, so my name is actually Sam but your people turned me into a monster. I am not going to spare them for what they did. I might be old but I will, at any cost, kill all of the monsters, and I will do anything to accomplish my goal. I will challenge them to a war and will create my own army.

AXCI: You are absolutely right, but through war you will lose, so no point in doing that. I will tell you the plan I had thought of.

OLD MAN: Ok, tell me.

AXCI: All the powers lie with the magical hippo. But once it moves from the golden emblem, all his powers will go back to God and everything will come back to normal. Though, not even a genius can move the hippo from it's place.

OLD MAN: Not a genius, but someone smarter than a genius could do it right. God, the creator of this universe, is the smartest, fastest, strongest of all. He may not have his powers but he still has his brain. He can definitely help us. We will go down to the dungeons and talk to him. And I was a scientist once, so even I might have some ideas. Let's go.

AXCI: Wow, what a great idea! I think even that might work.

(They go to the dungeons to meet God)

Axci and the old man tell Him their whole story. And then, God says, "I have been trapped here since 200 years and I had lost hope of the fact that maybe someone would come and free me from here but I believe in you." So God tells them that if they take the hair of every monster, even the hippo's, and mix it all in a potion, it will cause an explosion which will cause all the buildings to collapse. And if this explosion takes place near the emblem,the hippo will fall and die. And the powers would then go back to Him. He also gave them the recipe of the potion and told them that Docve was his friend, who was an idiot, and so would help them in making the potion.

Together, they decided that since the following day was Danner, while serving everybody drinks, they will pluck the hair of every monster; even the hippo's. Axci and the old man thanked God and left, to meet Docve.

So that night, Axci and the old man visited Docve who was the idiot of the city of Xaliar itself. They told him about the plan which they had thought of. Docve agreed with them and said, "Don't worry, the potion will be ready by tomorrow."

Axci and the old man thanked him for his help

and meanwhile, gathered some other monsters to help them with the work of plucking the hair the following day.

(The next morning, Sam and Axci left for MISSION CHANGE.)

All the monsters started arriving at the party which was held at MONQUET which was an open area near the golden emblem of powers. So, as soon as everybody came, their plan was to get set, go! One by one, the monsters served the guests drinks and plucked out their hair, and their plan appeared to be working, and was in full action.

After everybody's hair was collected, the only hair left was that of the hippo's. So Axci, with a lot of courage, went along with one of the monsters, holding a tray in his hand. He was trembling with fear but then, he remembered the face of God, and putting a smile on his face, hiding the fear, walked up to the hippo. While he was serving the drink, he started sweating and the hippo asked him, "Want to kill me do you?" Axci froze! But to his surprise the hippo burst out laughing and said, "I was joking, chill!" Axci sighed a sigh of relief.

While Axci was talking to the hippo, one of the monsters plucked the hippo's hair from behind.

Then, after taking his hair, they called Docve and he brought the potion with him. All of them threw their hair and the hair of the other monsters, including the hippo's, into the cauldron. Then, they placed the cauldron near the golden emblem of powers. When the hippo saw the smoke coming out of the cauldron, he started screaming, "AAAAAAA-AAAAAA!!"

And before he could stop screaming, the cauldron exploded and the hippo, including all the monsters, died.

The dungeon's gates burst open and God came out and He got back his powers.

And with a flick of His finger, God created his own peaceful, happy world where the monsters became humans and lived in the world above, in peace and happiness.

HOME SWEET HOME

This story is the greatest story of all times in the Marine kingdom.

It was the time of the fishing season, so the king whose name was Maring, had warned all the animals to stay inside their homes. It was a red alert for all animals in the ocean.

Everyone listened to their king and stayed inside their homes.

But the next day, when everyone woke up, they saw that Toto - the turtle was missing.

His father was hissing and pissing.

His mother was scared and crying,

 They tried to find him, and kept trying and trying.

But Toto, the turtle, was nowhere to be found,

He was lost in all this sound.

Instead, Toto, the turtle was crawling between toes,

and climbing over mountains that had a mouth, eyes, and nose.

His mind was scowling,

 His stomach was twitching and starving.

So he entered a cafe and started jumping up and down on the tables, while stealing food along the way.

He jumped onto the shoulder of a lady who was carrying a tray.

He leaped over a car and two,

and through the skies like a bird he flew.

He crashed into a building,

swinging on to a branch; it felt like he was on a parachute and was gliding.

And after the adventure was over,

he wanted to stay here forever.

The turtle was loving it here and was extremely glad that he had taken a risk and had come out to experience this amazing world that had beholden him. He never wanted to leave from here. He might have been born somewhere else, but he had lost his heart over here. He knew that he would always be happy here.

Toto could not stop grinning and his life felt like that of an imposter. He was extremely happy.

As he was thanking God and was walking along, suddenly, a muddy old boot blocked his way. The turtle moved to the left and the right but the boot blocked its path. The turtle looked up and he saw:

A freckled boy with a funny look on his face,

who was carrying a small case.

As soon as he opened his mouth, his tiny little yellow teeth could be seen.

Toto wanted to run away and was very keen.

The boy gave Toto a mean look,

and within the flick of a second, Toto was taken.

The turtle looked for help around,

but no one was to be found.

The turtle was extremely scared and tried to squirm away from the greasy and fat hands of the boy, but the boy held him tightly. The turtle felt disgusted, afraid, angry at the boy, and anxious about what was going to happen to him, next. Whether he will be beheaded or cooked in a frying pan. Thinking of it gave him the chills. And seeing him struggle, the boy started to laugh.

After a long walk, the boy took him to his home and closed him in a weird looking box. Toto started to cry and missed his mother. He was trapped within four walls and felt extremely blue. He felt miserable of the fact that he had not listened to his elders and had come out into this mixed-up world. The boy closed the door and left him alone. Toto felt abandoned and he had no one to hold.

That day, Toto spent the whole day crying from pain and misery. The next day, the boy took Toto to his school. He held him up with one leg and showed him to all his friends, as if he was a toy. Then at lunch, he threw Toto in the dustbin and tossed him around as if he was a basketball.

After this long and disturbing day, Toto knew that he had made the biggest mistake of his life by leaving his home and coming here.

It was late at night,

and it was a beautiful sight.

The moon was glistening,

and a slow breeze was blowing.

The night stirred,

and no sound was to be heard.

But Toto was shedding tears,

and thinking about it gave him the fears.

It was almost midnight and everyone was fast asleep. Toto looked to the left and saw that the window was open. Hope arose. And Toto thought he could escape. He burst open the cage door with a flick of his nail and scurried off to the open window. He flew through the window and felt like a hero. But suddenly, there was an end to that joy as he was stuck in the window. He tried pushing and moving but he couldn't move. Just then, a bird came to his rescue. The bird pulled and pulled and Toto pushed and pushed and finally, he was out. He climbed onto the back of the bird and flew past the moon into the shining sky. He felt like a superhero. The bird dropped him down and Toto thanked the bird for if it weren't for him, he wouldn't have been able to escape. Without wasting any time, he crossed the rocky roads, long valleys and scurried off to the ocean, swimming straight to his house. All of a sudden, he was caught by something. When he turned around, he saw that his body was bound by a fish hook. A sudden shock of danger flowed through his body. A fisherman had caught him. The turtle couldn't bear it, first the boy and now this! He kept on telling himself that this horrifying and terrible day will be over soon. This night could not get any worse for him. The fisherman removed the hook off him and put him in a net. As the turtle was cursing his future, he thought of an idea. He remembered that he could call out to Ann and Vann, his best friends. They had a special call which they made when any one of them was in trouble and needed each other's help. They just had to call out "CLOWN" and the others would come to the rescue. So, on top of his voice, Toto shouted out loud, "CLOOOOOOWN". The fisherman thought the turtle had gone mad, so he turned the other way and continued fishing. Within a second, Ann and Vann were right there and they saw Toto trapped in the net. Toto asked them to get everyone to come and save him. So they went to call everyone else. Time passed by, and to Toto's surprise, Ann and Vann came, not alone, but had brought the whole kingdom with them; his mom and dad as well. They all came and started chewing on the net while the fisherman was fishing on the other side of the boat. And after a lot of hard work, they managed to create a hole in the net, and Toto came out. His mother wrapped him in her arms and softly spoke into his ear, "Are you okay, my love?" They hugged and they kissed until it was dawn, and were glad that they were back together. Then his mother shouted at him and gave him her angry look, but Toto had never been so happy before, as he was now, to see his mother's angry look. And from that day onwards, he realized that there is no other place like home.

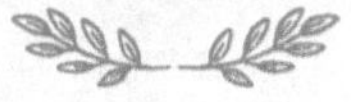

HUARO - THE HALF-HUMAN AND HALF-DINOSAUR

Have you ever wondered if there were no humans on Earth, what would it look like? Who would be there?

Let me give you a sneak peek of such a world.

This goes back to thousands and thousands of years, when there were no humans; instead, there were DIIIIIIINNNNOOOSSSAAAUUURRRSS!!

This is the story of a half-human and half-Dinosaur that changes the map of the world of dinosaurs.

DIORAUS was their world which was as green and lush as a parrot.

They used to eat small insects and grass instead of vegetables.

There were T-rexes, Stegosauruses and whatnot.

And with each other, they very often fought.

So everything was going on as usual. But one night, an egg cracked open and out came a tiny baby who held the fate of all the dinosaurs.

In the morning, when everybody came to see that bundle of joy, they saw that:

His face wasn't blue or pink; neither was he green.

His face was a colour that none of them had ever seen.

It was a similar colour to the ball that glowed up in the sky,

his head had something growing out of it like fields of brown grass and they wanted to understand what it was and wanted to try.

All of them were astonished to see such a creature,

whose head was different and from down, he had a blue tale popping out. Nobody had ever seen such a half-head and half-tail feature.

He had four legs like a dinosaur and had a blue body, sparks, and tail.

But his head was somewhat different, nobody could understand what he was and were a total fail.

Everybody said that he was a curse and so he was named HUARO, as he was half-human and half-dinosaur. It was quite confusing as to why he had turned out like this.

This had happened because his mother had gone

to the JUNGLE OF DARK which was a forbidden area. After all, black magic happened there! When she went to explore it, she got very hungry and picked fruit from there. That fruit held magical powers that had side effects on her child.

Huaro's parents were happy with their baby just the way he was! But not every dinosaur thought like that. As time passed by, he and the other cubs grew up. But none of the cubs played with him. They all pushed him aside as he never looked like them. Although, he was the favorite of his mother and father, he could never make any friends as whenever he went out to play, nobody played with him; instead, they made fun of him. Huaro felt very lonely and abandoned. He was extremely sad. He wished that he also looked like all the other dinosaurs. But he had a special gift which was granted to him, that would change the fate of all the dinosaurs. This was the only reason for his birth.

Huaro was the smartest but was the least fast. He couldn't roar like a dinosaur, but could solve anything. This was his special spark.

In time, all the dinosaurs grew up, including Huaro. They still didn't stop discriminating against him. Huaro couldn't take it anymore. He was sick to death with people treating him like this. He thought to himself, "I need to think of a way so that these dinosaurs start to like me."

Since he was half-human, he had the smartest brain. The next morning, he built a house for himself. Every brick he placed was a ray of hope for him as he thought that if he taught all the other dinosaurs inventions like this which they had never seen or even heard about, they would start to like him.

Huaro was very sure that everybody would come and like it, but unfortunately, that was not the case. Huaro kept waiting the whole day until midnight for the dinosaurs to come and ask him about his new invention, but nobody came as they did not want to talk to Huaro.

Huaro was extremely disappointed and sad. He went to bed thinking that he was a complete failure.

But the next day, when he woke up he heard a lot

of commotion outside his house. He thought that the time had come for everybody to throw him out of there. He could already imagine it.

But with trembling hands when he opened the gate, all the dinosaurs poured in and pleaded him to teach them too, about his new invention.

Huaro put a grin on his face and set to work. That was the turning point in his life.

 He taught the dinosaurs how to build a house. All the dinosaurs came and learned from him and only the king was left. He was quite stubborn, but then he too came to Huaro and asked him for forgiveness for the way Huaro had been treated before. Huaro forgave him and from that day on, everybody started loving Huaro. Huaro taught them how to make more and more inventions as he showed them how to grow fruits and vegetables by farming. He also taught them how to make coffee and toffee, etc. Dioraus was no longer a world of grass; instead, it was fully developed. It had buildings here and there, trains, cars, and airplanes moving all over the place. All thanks to Huaro! But since he was also half-dinosaur, he slept, ate, and talked like dinosaurs, so a part of him had the genius brain and on the other hand, he was a dinosaur by heart. He was eventually crowned the king. From that day on, nothing remained the same in Dioraus - where dinosaurs lived in a world like humans. And the fate of all the coming generations of dinosaurs changed thereafter because they were going to have a world which would be full of surprises and excitement.

Well, we never know; maybe even our ancestors were like HUARO.

Also, Huaro's story reminds us that life may have thrown him around, but finally, one point changed the map of his life. So you never know what turning point life might give you.

MIX-UP

Our brain is a solar system, where the Sun which is the biggest star and the main source of light, is happiness. The other planets revolving around it are our other emotions. For example, Mercury is mean, Earth is exciting, Jupiter is jealous, Saturn is fearful, and so on and so forth. Well, this story is about a 10-year-old girl, Sara.

Her brain is also a solar system, like everyone else's, but from time to time, Sara's body twitches and she gets a shock throughout her body. She thinks that it must have happened due to the cold weather. But she is wrong! Do you know what has happened? Do you know?? Saturn and the Sun got merged. The emotions of happiness and fear got merged. Everything was about to change in her life. Let us see the side effects of this mix-up. When Sara went to school after her vacation, she had gym class. The gym teacher had arranged for an obstacle course in the lawn. When it was Sara's turn, she started laughing and said, "I am so scared. I do not want to do this, please. I am afraid." Then she started crying loudly and started shouting, "I am so happy, I am so glad."

The teacher and all the other kids were absolutely amazed and shocked at her behavior, since nobody knew about the mix-up!

When it was lunchtime, Sara ran into one of her friends, but out of fear she started running and was shouting, "happy to see you." On one hand, she was scared and was running, while on the other hand, she was shouting - happy to see you?? Everyone was dismayed by her behaviour.

After Sara returned home, she saw her mother and gasped and crept towards her, stared her in the face, and ran quickly shouting, "School is awesome. I had a lot of fun."

At night when she was sleeping, she had a dream and started laughing loudly and everyone woke up and ran to her room thinking she was in trouble. But when they went there, they saw her laughing. They asked her what had happened and she said that she saw a black monster eating her. Her parents were perturbed by her behaviour and decided to talk to the principal of the school.

The next morning when they went to the principal's office, Sara saw the solar system kept in her room. Her attention went on to the Sun and Earth. Then her body twitched and there was a shock in her brain again. This time, the Sun and Earth merged. That means happiness was merged with excitement. The next morning when Sara went back to her school, her teacher said that he was taking a surprise test. While everyone was moaning and whining, Sara said, "I am so happy we are having a test. YAY! I am so excited." All the students were curious due to the fact that Sara was never a bright student and she hated tests, but suddenly she was acting so weird! Then, when Sara was in her math class, one of her friends told her that her grandfather passed away. And Sara immediately replied,"I am so happy to hear this news. This is so exciting. Congrats!" Her friend was very upset and left from there, weeping. Sara did not understand as to why her friend had left. Her friend came to give Sara another chance and showed Sara her marksheet on which there was a huge red egg. She had failed. Sara said,"Oh we should throw a party for this, a huge celebration. It must be such a proud day for you."

After that day, whenever Sara saw a solar system somewhere, the system in her brain would change.

NO LOGIC, ONLY MAGIC!

I am sure that all of us love some movie character or the other. A character whom we relate to or resemble. So, here I am, bringing to you the movie world that has come alive!!

All the movie characters have come to life, and this is the breaking news everywhere! Nobody knows how this magic has happened but it is not a dream; it is reality. This is sure to be a magical, adventurous, fantasy-filled, and historical adventure.

On one street, the Marvel stars have come to play. Spiderman is swaying from one pole to the other. Iron Man is showing off his attire to all of his fans, while Captain Marvel is showing off his shield. And amidst all of this, is the sound of thousands and thousands of screaming fans. They are like cats, just wanting to gobble up all of them.

This was a glimpse of the action world, but now let us step into the world of magic and fantasy!

Beware 'cause the potterheads are back. The final battle between Harry and his team versus 'He who should not be named(Lord Voldemort)'. Lights are crashing everywhere. The atmosphere is all purple, blue, and black. Where the tension is rising, the voices of thousands of screaming, mad fans is more than the noise of the spells being cast. The old and the young; everyone has come to see their idols.

While the background is a bit dark, we shall go on an animated journey.

Shrek, his beautiful wife, and his loyal donkey are travelling in their Pumpkin chariot. They are off to the kingdom of 'Happily Ever After'.

This was a peek into this world, which is quite amazing.

So, Harry is a very famous character in the whole world. Thousands of fans were standing in line just to see and meet him. Everyone was thrilled and excited. But among those potterheads was a boy, Toffa.

Everybody in line gets to meet Harry and all the other people as well. After waiting for long, finally, Toffa gets the chance to meet his idol. He shakes hands with Harry and tells him that he wished he could be famous like Harry and have an incredible life, like his. The boy is dreaming of the perfect life just when Harry's voice breaks in. He says, "You want to have a life like me? I would trade anything to have a normal life. It is not quite easy being in my shoes." The boy says, "Well, you are a wizard, right? So why don't we exchange our lives for one day and both of our dreams will be fulfilled." "Great," exclaims Harry.

After everybody is done with, Harry and the boy meet on an isolated street and the magic happens. Using his powers, Harry and the boy exchange lives.

Both of them were gleeful but what they did not know was that after this moment, the lives of both of them were going to change.

After they exchanged their lives for a day, they parted ways.

Harry went to the boy's house while the boy went to the cottage where Harry and his colleagues were staying.

The boy took advantage of the luxuries in Harry's life. The best house, best food, and best life. His room was amazing with a comfy bed and was very spacious. The living room was also very huge. It had a huge sofa with a LED television in front of it. The boy was grinning widely with joy. At his house, there were fixed timings for everything but over here, he could do whatever he wanted, whenever he wanted. He was as free as a bird. He was living the dream! All of it was extremely fun and thrilling. Although he was having a perfect day, he was, after all, missing his family and his small but sweet house. He was happy that this arrangement was only for one day. He would get to live part of his dream and then, he would go back to his normal life.

Well, we have seen the boy's life, but let us take a peek into the boy's, now Harry's life.

Harry was quite tired with all the fans and the publicity around him. He was tired of the media and just wanted to have his personal space, which he hoped he would get from this one day.

As we all know, Harry was an orphan but here, he got a family for free! The boy's mom, dad, sister, and a cute dog. He loved having a family. He enjoyed all the love and attention he got. He had never felt this special before. And he never wanted to go back to his busy life. Over here, he always had his own space and private life. It was quiet and peaceful instead of the screams of thousands of fans. He could find his happy place and be living a life he had only imagined. He felt very fortunate to get such an opportunity.

The next day, the boy and he met on the same street. The boy asked him to change them back and he closed his eyes. After a few seconds, he opened his eyes again, but he was still Harry! He once again asked Harry to change him back, and closed his eyes. They both tried it a lot of times but nothing happened. The boy looked quite confused. So Harry told him that he knew that it was the boy's dream to have a life like his and he must have been quite happy and that Harry was quite happy too, so the previous night he had cast a spell by which they would be stuck in each other's lives or bodies forever. The boy's jaw was open wide. His face turned red and he was outraged. He barked at Harry, "How dare you! You never even asked me before taking such a decision. This will change my whole life. Not once did you consult me. I was happy with your life.

But the truth is, I am not used to all of this luxury and I was missing my family and wanted my life back. But you never even asked me. How could you?"

Harry felt very ashamed of himself. He had thought that the boy was very happy but he never even asked him, and now, the spell could not be reversed and they both were stuck in each other's lives forever.

Toffa was extremely disheartened and blue. As he started to cry, his tears fell on Harry's wand which was in his hand. That second, both of them saw a pink cloud form above them and they fainted. When they woke up, the boy was turning away when he looked down and saw that instead of Harry's shoes, he was wearing his shoes. He turned around to give the shoes when he saw that Harry was Harry! They were supposed to be in each other's bodies but as the boy's tear had fallen on the wand, the magic was reversed and they both had gotten back into their bodies. The boy screamed with happiness when Harry woke up and saw what had happened. Both of them hugged each other and started dancing. Sometimes there is no logic, only magic.

DREAMS

All of us are born for a reason. And while we are here, one thing common in all of us is that we all dream. All of us dream. Do you know how we get these inspiring thoughts? Well, let us get a glimpse of them.

That mighty power that rests above us in the clouds is the one who writes these dreams for us, and he puts them into packages and then they are parcelled into our brains and that is how we dream and spend our whole lives fulfilling them. But not all dreams turn out right.

Here's what happened. Heaven was in its place. The mighty waters were flowing at the perfect speed. The light flowers were blossoming beautifully. Everything was where it was supposed to be and the place was in tranquility.

The Gods were busy packing dreams for everyone, but suddenly, Wise - the elephant, came crashing in and threw everything around. It took a lot of people to calm him down. Although the things were put back in order, nobody had realized that on the way, Wise had crashed into the table which had piles of dreams - one plie for nice people and another for naughty people. One of the packages fell down and one of the caretakers, without noticing, mixed up a dream.

After a while, Sade - the caretaker, went to the two chutes to parcel the dreams according to the two piles. And as nobody noticed, one of the nice people's dreams got mixed up with one of the naughty people's dreams.

It will take some time for the parcels to reach the respective people so let us have a look below.

The parcels which got exchanged belonged to Nara and Sawa.

Nara was a very nice and down to earth girl, for whom the dream was to become a great and sweet person and spread affection to everyone.

But her dream got exchanged with that of Sawa. Oh, Sawa! He was the most notorious person you could ever meet. He was a delinquent and was very disobedient. He was also very rude, and for him the dream was to talk rudely to everyone and to not listen. He was not to study, but play video games all day. God had written this dream for him as he wanted to teach him a lesson. After behaving like this, everybody would scold him and then, he would finally become a good man. Both dreams were a good fit for both of these people, according to their personalities. But they got exchanged, so Nara would have to dream Sawa's dream and Sawa would have to dream Nara's dream.

Both of them knew each other very well and were the best of friends.

But unfortunately, their dreams got exchanged. So let us see what ruckus this led to.

After a tiring day, both of them went to their houses and slept. And that is when they saw a dream.

The next morning, when Nara and Sawa went to school, Nara had completely changed. As soon as she stepped in, the other kids greeted her but instead, she just pushed them aside. Everyone was dismayed by her behaviour. When the teacher arrived, Nara shouted and screamed at her. During lunchtime, she caught Dose by his collar and smashed him into a pillar. And when she was called to the principal's office, she broke some glass objects and started dancing on the table, showing no respect. Well, after that dream, all of this was bound to happen. While everyone was shocked at Nara's behaviour, there was more astonishment at Sawa's behaviour. The rude and bad one started distributing roses to everyone and started hugging them. He talked to everyone politely and sat with a lot of kids and listened to their problems and even helped them. From the rude-talker, he had become the well-wisher. Everyone was shocked by their unexpected behavioural changes.

Not only humans, but even God! He could see whatever was going on down there. Therefore, he decided to sort this whole mess out.

He observed the way both Nara and Sawa were behaving. And he could not understand what to do. On one hand, he was very happy for Sawa as he had changed a lot, but on the other hand, he was not quite proud of what was happening to Nara.

But then he thought that they must have got the

wrong dreams, but that they are still themselves. They might be fulfilling their dream but they could still realize what was right or wrong for them. They might be determined and influenced in their dream, but they still use their brain and they can surely figure it out; plus, it will be a good exercise for them.

And after several days went by like this, nothing really changed. And God was not happy with that. So he decided to take a firm decision, and the next day, Nara apologized to all her teachers and classmates. She did not have a perfect explanation for everything but she managed to untangle all the tangles she had created over those past few days. What happened was that God went into Nara's dreams and showed her what she was doing wrong. And that tiny lesson changed the mess that she was in and everything was back to perfect again.

He made a good decision that day, but he also took a new decision to not create any dreams, because he saw what happened when he wrote dreams for everyone. Sometimes, they went well and sometimes they ended up ruining people's lives. So he wanted the people themselves to dream what they wanted to do and spend their lives working on their dreams. It would also be a good encouragement for them. So from that day on, God was not responsible for any dreams and the people dreamed themselves and the world was a balanced place to live in.

Sawa, of course, was treating everybody like it was Valentine's Day!

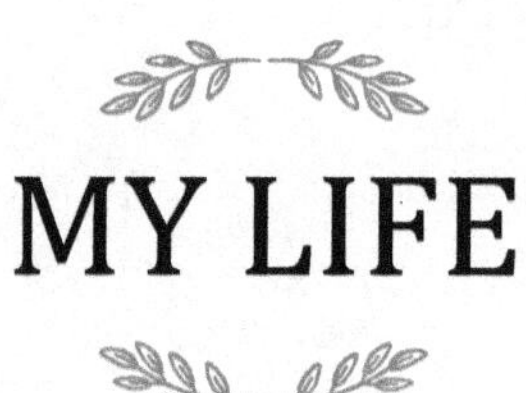

MY LIFE

My life has been quite difficult as a mouse.

I might be talking like a human right now … well, actually … I do talk like a human even while being a mouse.

I wish that I do not become human in any of my future births.

I was once a perfect, non-talking, stinking, rotten, but happy mouse, and then, one drink changed the map of my life. I was living with my family in the corner of a lab belonging to the famous scientist Mr Dontill. He did not know we existed and for us, he did not exist. Our life was as perfect as a large feast, but then, one day one of Dontill's potions had fallen and he did not realize that. And being a kid, I was quite fascinated and galvanized by that orange, bubbly liquid so I ran towards it and drank some of it. That was when I heard the door creak and I scurried off to my hole.

I began telling my mother what happened in the room, in our mouse language. But then, suddenly, I started talking like humans. I was speaking in words and sentences. Oh my God!! I could not understand anything. All the mice crawled up to me and started staring at me with their big, black, and scary eyes. But I was clueless and bewildered as to what was happening.

Everybody was terrified and I was sweating out of fear. As I was trying to think and converse like the "humans" with the other mice, just then, the scientist heard us and he stuck his hand into our hole. Everyone started panicking and running as if that hand was a gun and it would shoot all of them. But that big and slimy hand of the scientist caught me by the tail. And then, I told him to let go of me, but he started to shout and jump with glee. He was thrilled that his potion had worked. He had made this potion by which animals could talk like humans, and he had dropped this potion that I drank up. Ever since, I have been talking like the "humans".

What a terrible thing! My life was ruined by that potion. But it was also the start of a new life because, from that day on, the scientist promised to give me the luxuries of life if I became his companion and help him in his research work only for a couple of days. Well, it was a win-win from any angle you saw it, and come on, who could refuse such an offer? So, I went for it.

Dontill made a whole room for me. It had a soft and comfortable bed, and you would not believe it, but it had an obstacle course for me to run and jump about and have fun. As a small and naïve mouse, I found all of this very lavish and royal.

It felt mesmerizing and heart-warming to have such luxuries in my life.

When I climbed down the stairs, I saw the scientist and asked him for food. Then, within a second, somebody picked me up and carried me to a small table with a huge feast laid out just for me. At first, I was appalled. But then, I saw cheese and the last thing I remember was that I ate every piece of cheese on the table.

Dontill had made me realize what an amazing brain I had to not refuse such an offer.

But as days passed by, I was starting to miss my family, my mom. And by now, Dontill had also done a lot of research and it was about time. So I went to him and told him that it had been quite some time since I had seen my mom and that he had done a lot of research already. So I said, "Thank you for your enlightenment but I will be going now." As soon as I kept my foot one step forward, the scientist caught me by my tail and told me that our deal was forever. I can never go, visit my mom, and that I have to stay with him forever. But I had thought that it was only for a few days, according to what the scientist had earlier said. Then, somebody picked me up and put me into a cage. I was terrified, petrified, and tired. This time, no fancy room, no fancy anything; the only thing I fancied was my breathing. I was shoved into a dark place. I felt isolated and secluded. But who could help me? Just then, at the window, I saw a pink ribbon popping out, and my mom was climbing on to it. Oh, my mom!! I felt like running up to her and sinking in her arms. She came to me and hugged me through the cage. "Mom power!" I almost cried out. Then she called my dad and as he had very sharp nails he opened the lock of my cage and I could come out. I wrapped myself in their arms. I told them whatever had happened until then. I now saw all the other mice climbing up the ribbon. I was befuddled, but just then, my mom said that we were going to teach the scientist a lesson. She said that she had come to the scientist's house to talk to me when she heard my conversation with him, and had followed me so that she could get the army to teach the brat a lesson.

My mom shouted out loud, "Till cheese's (our favorite dish) end, Mouse Army defend."

All of us ran to his room and started jumping on the cups and plates. We broke everything. Many mice climbed onto the fan and it came down, crashing on the table. We started nibbling on the food and we even made a catapult with a spoon and a band, now shooting food onto the faces of the scientist and his servants. It was a ruckus! They started running around and we got into their shirts and pants and started tickling them. Then, we finally came closer to the scientist. We scratched his nose and mouth and all the mice climbed onto him and in his clothes, and it was a major blast down! And Fatty, the mouse, farted in his mouth and the scientist was unconscious in a second.

That was the best day of my life. That was because it was the only day when I won against the humans.

Even though I continued to talk like the humans, I was finally with my family and I was happy and healthy.

Although coming across the scientist was a huge mistake, I learned a lot of things from that incident in my life.

BOOK LOVER
FOREVER

Fedrami, the idol of Turkytown. The shine and pride of Turkytown.

Let me tell you about her story. She did not like reading books at all. But as she was not well educated, she could not get a job anywhere. But finally, the day that changed her life had arrived. One of the librarians of a library nearby, gave Fedrami the job of cleaning the library.

She was very grateful for the job. The next day, she went to the library and started on her job. Several months passed by like this. But one day, Turkytown faced a huge thunderstorm. Buildings fell, trees crashed onto the ground with a boom. Fires blazed atop several rooftops. Many people locked themselves in their homes. Screams could be heard from far away. But Fedrami was stuck at the library as the roads were jammed with water. She was terrified and the voices of people in her mind would not fade away. And while Fedrami was thinking away, there was a sudden knock on the door. Fedrami's heart skipped a beat. She was horrified as to who might be standing outside the door. The knocking didn't stop and then

Fedrami got up, and she slowly crept towards the door. Her heart was thumping hard in her chest and her heartbeat could be heard from a mile away. With a heavy heart, her cold her hands, grasped the handle tightly and closing her eyes, she pressed the handle downwards and very slowly opened the door. She could not hear any noise, and sweating now, she opened a part of her eyelid but could not see anybody at the door. She looked around and gasped. A book jumped in front of her face. He was as fat as the librarian and as colorful as a butterfly and he had eyes like that of a human, a nose like a human, a mouth like a human; and if that was not enough, he had hands and legs like a human. Butttt he was on fiiiiiireeeeeee!! His pages were burning and then the most drastic thing happened. He talked and said, "Hi, sorry to disturb, but I and my friends here(from behind him, some more books came out) have got fire on some of our pages, so can you please help us?" Having a kind heart, Fedrami got a towel and started to blow out the fire. While blowing out the fire, she had a glance at one or two pages and started reading a few lines; and by the time she reached the end of the page, she was curious to read more. But then she realized that some of the pages were burnt and she could not read some more. The next day, after the petrifying storm, Fedrami picked up a book from the library and started reading it. She developed a lot of keenness and was eager to read more. Every day, she used to take a book home and for the entire evening, she would sit with a cup of coffee and just read the book. Like this, she kept on reading for many months, and very soon she had read almost all the books in the library; and that too, books from all sections like biography, autobiography, fiction, non-fiction, etc. It was surprising as Fedrami hated books, but now she had read almost all the books in the library.

She now decided that instead of reading books, she would write one. So in the evening, when everyone had left, she gathered some papers, a stapler and a pencil from the librarian's desk, and she started writing. After a lot of hard work and many days later, she had finally finished writing her first book. She felt very proud of herself. The next morning, she sneakily kept her book on the fiction shelf. Many children came and saw the book. They picked it up and started reading it. Fedrami was delighted to see that children liked her book. One of the mothers of the kids told the librarian that her kid loved reading the book 'Cheese on the go!' and wanted more books of the author. 'Cheese on the go!' was the first creation of Fedrami. She did not want anybody to know that she had written the book as she was very shy. So in the book, she had written the author's name as 'Book lover forever'. Yet again, a busy day started at the library when Fedrami's eyes noticed a letter. That letter was written to 'Book lover forever' which was her, and it said that everybody at the library wanted to meet this author and they were keen to receive more books from her. So Fedrami once again got some supplies from the librarian's desk, and all night she kept cutting, stapling, sharpening, and writing. When everyone came rushing into the library the next day, they saw that there was a small table upon which was taped a note which said, "HERE IS THE AUTHOR, START WRITING." There were many small, blank books kept beside the note, along with some pencils. So the kids picked up those books and started writing stories and they added to the world of imagination. There was a shelf made where the books of the kids were displayed. Fedrami felt pleased that she had passed on that inspiration and motivation to write, to the children. And on the side, there was also a shelf created separately for Ms. Book lover forever's books. She had written many books by now.

I have also written this book by taking inspiration from Fedrami, and so should you!